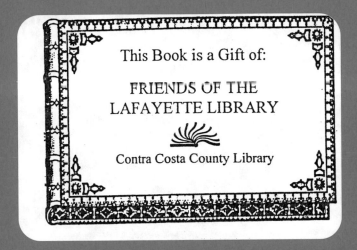

TOOTH FAIRY'S FIRST NIGHT

For Ellen, editor and friend
—A.B.

To Leanne, Ciara, and Jessica
—J.B.

Carolrhoda Books, Inc.
A division of Lerner Publishing Group, Inc.
241 First Avenue North
Minneapolis, MN 55401 U.S.A.

Website address: www.lernerbooks.com

Library of Congress Cataloging-in-Publication Data

Bowen, Anne, 1952-
  Tooth fairy's first night / by Anne Bowen ; illustrations by Jon Berkeley.
    p. cm.
  Summary: Sally the tooth fairy's first day on the job is a challenge when
a toothless little girl hides her tooth and makes Sally follow a series of
clues to find it.
  ISBN-13: 978-1-57505-753-8 (lib. bdg. : alk. paper)
  ISBN-10: 1-57505-753-0 (lib. bdg. : alk. paper)
  [1. Tooth fairy--Fiction. 2. Treasure hunt (Game)--Fiction.] I. Berkeley,
Jon, ill. II. Title.
PZ7.B671945To 2005
[E]--dc22
                                        2004006594

Manufactured in the United States of America
5 6 7 8 9 10 — JR — 12 11 10 09 08 07

TOOTH FAIRY'S FIRST NIGHT

Anne Bowen • illustrations by Jon Berkeley

Carolrhoda Books • Minneapolis • New York

 For as long as she could remember, Sally wanted to be a tooth fairy, just like her mama and grandma and great-grandma before her.

On the night of her seventh birthday, Mama presented Sally with her very own tooth fairy purse.

"Tonight you must get your first tooth," said Mama.

"With that first tooth, you will become an official tooth fairy," said Grandma.

"We know you will follow in the tradition of all great tooth fairies," Great-Grandma told her.

Sally flittered.

She fluttered.

She wrapped her wings around herself in one big hug.

"I will be the BEST tooth fairy in the world!" she promised.

"Remember, a good tooth fairy is always patient," said Mama.

"A good tooth fairy always looks on the bright side of things," said Grandma.

"A good tooth fairy always gets her tooth," said Great-Grandma.

"And don't forget," they called, as Sally flew into the night, "you must never, ever wake a sleeping child."

Sally's first tooth belonged to Miranda Kay Michaels. Her tooth had fallen out just that morning, right after biting into a Taffy Doodle at recess.

When Sally arrived at Miranda Kay's house, she wriggled through a crack beneath the front door and sat down in the darkness to catch her breath. She pulled out her flashlight and map, searching for Miranda's room.

"It should be down the hall, last door on the left," Sally whispered.

"Now I just need to find that tooth, and I'll be on my way."

Slowly,
 carefully,
  Sally reached beneath
  Miranda Kay's pillow.

"Oh, no," Sally thought, "what is this?"

Sally pulled out a pink envelope
and read the letter inside:

Dear Tooth Fairy
My friend Emily says you are not
~~reel~~ real, but my friend Sam
says you are. He saw you once
flying out his bedroom window.

I want to know who is right,
so I am hiding my tooth in
a very ~~secrit~~ secret place.
A place only a smart tooth
fairy can find.

Yours truly,
Miranda Kay Michaels

Sally's lip quivered. It trembled. "Mama and Grandma and Great-Grandma never said anything about a letter!"

A tiny tear trickled down her cheek.
Sally blew her nose—BRRONK—and whispered,
"A good tooth fairy
is always patient.
I AM a good tooth
fairy. I WILL find
that tooth!"

And then Sally noticed another piece of paper tucked inside the pink envelope:

Dear TF,
Here's your first clue:
This place is ~~for~~ your size
but too small for me.
You can eat cherry cupcakes
while sipping hot tea.

Sally thought
and thought
and then she thought harder.

"A dollhouse!"

Sally spotted a house just her size beneath the window. Inside, she flew up the stairs and down, flittering from one room to the next. At last, in the kitchen, Sally found what she was looking for—tiny chairs around a tiny table, set with tiny cups and a teapot. Inside one of the cups was . . .

another note
   but no tooth!

Sally's lower lip quivered. It trembled.
Then she read the note:

Sally took a deep breath and whispered, "A good
tooth fairy always looks on the bright side of things.
I AM a good tooth fairy. I WILL find that tooth!"

Sally thought
　　　and thought
　　　　　and then she thought harder.

"A piggy bank!"

Sally spotted a big, pink
pig in the corner of
Miranda Kay's room.

"This is going to be tight!"
she said, as she squeezed
down inside the pig.

Sally stumbled about in the
dark, bumping her shins on
several coins until she
remembered her flashlight.
The light brightened the inside
of the pig, making all the
pennies, nickels, and dimes
shimmer. Beneath
a fifty-cent coin,
Sally found . . .

another note
      but no tooth!

This time, Sally's
lower lip didn't quiver.
It didn't tremble.
Not even once.

"A good tooth fairy
always gets her tooth,"
she whispered, "and I'm
not leaving until I get mine!"

She read the note:

Sally thought
and thought
and then she thought harder.

"A kangaroo!"

Sally looked around the room and there, on Miranda Kay's bed, were stuffed animals everywhere. Right in the middle of all those animals was Miranda Kay, sound asleep.

"A good tooth fairy never, ever wakes a sleeping child," Sally reminded herself.

Sally flew from one animal to another. A black bear. Three tiny mice. A brown rabbit. But there was no kangaroo.

Sally plopped down on the pink nose of a cat to rest her wings and think.

Suddenly, the cat's whiskers twitched.
With one swipe of its paw, the cat
sent Sally flying up, up into the air.
She fell down, down, down onto
Miranda Kay's pillow, right
next to Miranda Kay's nose.

"Snort, sniffle, snuffle," snored Miranda Kay.

Sally held her breath.
"Please, don't wake up."

Sally crawled beneath the blankets
and there, snuggled against Miranda
Kay, was a soft, gray kangaroo.

Slowly,
 carefully,
  Sally reached inside
  the tiny pouch of the kangaroo.

And there it was — Miranda Kay's tooth!

Sally flittered.

She fluttered.

"A good tooth fairy always
gets her tooth. Now I really
am a tooth fairy!"

Sally placed something special beneath
Miranda Kay's pillow.

Then she flew into the night with her
first tooth tucked inside her purse.

Early the next morning, when Miranda Kay woke up, she reached under her pillow and found a note: